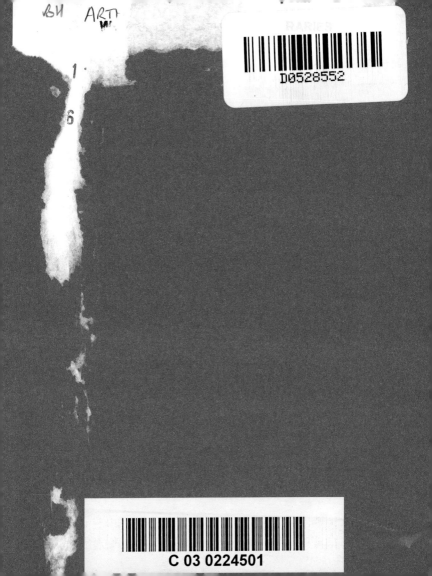

BH ARTI

1

6

D0528552

C 03 0224501

A Little Book of

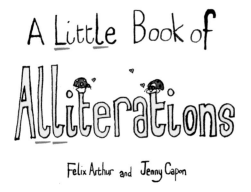

Alliterations

Felix Arthur and Jenny Capon

This book should be read aloud...

WEST DUNBARTONSHIRE LIBRARIES	
C 03 0224501	
HJ	28-Oct-2010
~~J421~~ JF	£5.99
BH	

Published in Great Britain by
Inside Pocket Publishing Limited

First published in Great Britain in 2010
Text © Felix Arthur, 2009

The right of Felix Arthur to be identified
as the author of this work has been asserted
in accordance with the
Copyright, Designs and Patents Act 1988

Illustrations © Jenny Capon

All rights reserved. No part of this publication may be
reproduced, stored in a retrieval system or transmitted
in any form or by any means, electronic, mechanical,
photocopying, recording or otherwise, without
the prior permission of the publishers.

A CIP catalogue record for this book is available from
the British Library

ISBN 978-0-9562315-5-0

Inside Pocket Publishing Limited Reg. No. 06580097

Printed and bound in Finland by WS Bookwell

www.insidepocket.co.uk

A
Little Book
of
Alliterations

by

Felix Arthur

with illustrations

by

Jenny Capon

INSIDE
POCKET

- **A** -

Awful Auntie Agatha
ate all of Arthur's
available apples

- B -

Boris the busy bee
bumbled into Betsy
in the barley

- C -

Claude the cockroach
could consume
countless crunchy carrots

- CH -

Chunky Charlie
cheerily chewed
chips and cheddar cheese

- D -

Donald dutifully
digested Della's
dreadful dumplings

- E -

Eagle-eyed Edward
envied Edna's
excellent eggs

- F -

Francois
the French farmer
frequently felt
frightfully funny

- G -

Gerald grew
green geraniums
in Gertie's
gorgeous garden

- H -

Hearty Harold
happily hopped
on Hilda's huge hippo

- I -

Ivan is irate
over Ivor's
increasingly idiotic
ideas

- J -

Judge John jumped
joyfully over
the jeering jury

- K -

Karen crept carefully
past Kevin's
creepy crypt

- L -

Lola loved looking
at Lanky Larry's
long legs

- M -

Morris made Meryl
measure Malcolm's
massive midriff

- N -

Noel knew nothing
about Nora's
night-time nibbles

- O -

Old Oscar outgrew
his only
orange overcoat

- P -

Percy produced
perfect pieces for
Peter's piano playing

- Q -

Quentin queried
Queen Carla's
quivering queue

- R -

Rugged Roger rode
roughly round
Red Ruby's riding ring

- S -

Silly Sally sat
sideways on
Selma's soft sofa

- Sh –

Shapely Sheila
shaved Shaun's
shaggy sheep

- T -

Tall Terry told
Tiny Timmy
terribly tearful tales

- Th –

Theo thought thoroughly
through Thelma's
third theory

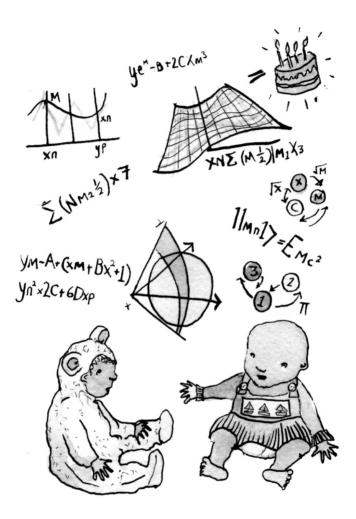

- U -

Uncle Unwin
utterly understood
Una's ugly utterances

- V -

Vapid Virginia
valued Victoria's
vibrant verses

- W -

Weird Willie
would willingly wear
whatever Wilma wished

- X -

Xeno expertly
examined
Xenon's xylophone

- Y -

Yasmin yawned
at Yorick's
yellow yacht

- Z -

Zorba the Zebra
zoomed zestfully
to the zoo

If you would like to submit
your own alliterations,
perhaps even with an illustration,
then please visit our website:

www.little-alliterations.com

We look forward to hearing from
you.

set by kkc